BIG**FAT**

First Date

Hedonist

Hedonist

CONTENTS

First Date   1

Author's Note   83

BIG FAT FIRST DATE

Late afternoon on a Monday, and I'm counting the minutes until five o'clock. Not that I have anything exciting to go home to, but today I can't wait to get out of the office. It's just been one of those days.

My repeated stares at the wall clock on the far end of the office are interrupted by an incessant buzz coming from my handbag. The boss isn't around, so I decide to risk it and check my phone.

Claire. Haven't heard from her in ages.

I grab my phone and make a quick escape into the hallway, out of earshot from my colleagues.

"Hey, girl!" I answer.

"Heyyy, Alison, hope I'm not disturbing?"

"I'm at work, but that's okay. How have you been?"

She's quiet for a moment. Yeah, this definitely isn't a friendly catch-up session. She wants something. I roll my eyes and brace myself for the inevitable.

"You know my new job…" she starts.

I try very hard to remember the details. "Producer for some TV thing, right?"

"Right. They promoted me to show-runner."

"Oh, wow! Congratulations." I try to sound genuine, but… *Why does Claire get the cool job, while I'm stuck here at the office, regretting my entire life?*

"Thanks…" She doesn't sound happy. *Okay, hit me already. What's the favour?*

"Did I ever tell you what the show was about?" she

asks.

"Umm… I don't recall. Some reality thing?"

"Right, right… Well they did tell us to keep it a secret, but I think…"

I take a deep breath. As much as it annoys me that she's only calling because she needs help, I do remember the good old days. Maybe she's just been too busy with her fancy new career to keep in touch with little old me.

"Claire. Just tell me already. What do you need?" I ask.

"Is it that obvious?"

Uhuh, yeah, pretty much. I don't say anything, though.

"Okay, well," Claire begins. "So it's a dating show, right? And now that they've promoted me, I really could use a win to prove myself."

"Okay…"

She chuckles awkwardly. "Wanna be on TV?"

I sigh. "No, not really. That's why you called? You want *me* on your dating show of all things? Did someone drop out or what?"

She's quiet again. "Well, it's a little more complicated than that."

Although I've already made up my mind, I'm still curious. What could be so complicated about a dumbass dating show?

"How so?"

"Let me ask you something else first. You still like big guys, right?" Claire asks.

I frown. "Do you still like underwear model types

with big dicks?" I counter.

"Dumb question, I get it. My point is... "

Yes, I would very much like to know what your point is now.

"I've got this guy on the show. And we tried to shoot his episode three times already. It's been a bit of a disaster."

"Don't tell me. You've got some sad loser on your show who doesn't know how to talk to women and you want me to come on and act all agreeable on TV so you can tick that one off your list, is that it?" I probe.

She's quiet again. "Why don't I just send you a few clips and you let me know what you think. But you have to promise not to share or post it anywhere. I could lose my job for this."

Now, I'm actually intrigued. "Fine. I promise."

"Right. You just watch them and call me back, okay?"

"Okay."

Some colleagues walk past on their way to the coffee machine. I pretend to be cool and smile at them. Who knows what Claire is about to send me? I'd better find some privacy.

My phone buzzes a few times to alert me of incoming messages, while I rush to the ladies room. I lock myself in a stall before checking my phone again.

With my sound set almost to zero, I open the first video.

The format of the show looks vaguely familiar, even if the clips are still a bit unpolished and the editing is rough. A flash restaurant where people meet for a blind date, the whole thing is recorded, etc. It's obvious where this is going.

But when the doors open and the man walks in, my mind goes blank.

He's gorgeous. Pushes all my buttons.

Firstly he's tall; over six feet for sure. And 'big' doesn't quite describe it. He's huge, four hundred, maybe four-fifty and it ain't muscle. His frame obscures the entire doorway behind him. That's enough to get me interested, but his face seals the deal.

Kind eyes, handsome features with a well-kept dark brown beard. He has the kind of face that could haunt many a wet dream of mine. I'm a sucker for a handsome face.

Then, there's his body language.

He shows vulnerability, whether purposefully or not. A realness that you don't often get to see - whether on TV or in real life. I'm hopelessly caught, like an insect in a sticky fly trap and can no longer look away.

He awkwardly heads to his seat, makes some small talk with the barman and waits. He's visibly nervous, which makes me want to reach out and tell him it's going to be okay. His discomfort of course is not helped by the barman's blatant stares.

That's just the person we see. How many more people; producers, assistants, camerapeople, etc. are doing the exact same thing off camera?

He isn't oblivious to it.

It's painful to watch him being put on the spot.

If he hates the attention, why did he go on the show,

though? It doesn't make a whole lot of sense to me.

But what's even worse is when the camera pans around and shows the doors again, a portly woman walks in. Even through the pounds of make-up she's caked onto her face, her expression of disappointment is clear as day. They shake hands, exchange a few awkward words, but it's already obvious that this isn't going anywhere.

She turns to someone out of frame and shakes her head.

The man just stands by, helplessly, and watches her with a pained expression on his face.

Then the video ends. I guess that was date number one, ending before it even began.

Ouch.

The next video starts off much the same, he comes into the restaurant, looking his usual awkward yet oh so sexy self. Sits down, makes the obligatory small talk with the bartender, and waits. Another woman enters; this one looks a lot friendlier at least. They greet each other and have a little exchange until someone shows them through to their table away from the bar.

I'm suckered into the scene in front of me and turn up the volume.

Conversation starts to flow. His baritone voice makes the hairs on the back of my neck stand up.

They share a bit of banter, he makes a few self deprecating jokes. She laughs, but it sounds a little forced to my ear. Or is that just because Claire already told me this isn't going to end well either?

Food starts to arrive, and they're still chatting. He asks about her; what does she do, that sort of thing. She answers, and while she's courteous, there's obviously something missing.

They do seem to get along, but it's clear to me that there's no chemistry there.

Meanwhile, I can't keep my eyes off him. His expressive brown eyes, his sensual lips.

He's trying so very hard to be charming, and it's working for me on every level.

But not for her.

I fast forward to the end of the video. The two of them are sitting on a couch together on a different part of the set. Above them, in cursive font, what has to be the name of the show; 'Sealed with a kiss'. Someone off-screen asks if they want to see each other again, and if so, to seal it with a kiss. *Cringe!*

It's the moment of truth. He says yes, he would love to see her again. She says…

The pause is long and awkward. Finally she says those most dreaded words: "I really like you, but just as a friend, perhaps."

The look on his face breaks my heart. I've decided he isn't the loser in this clip, *she* is.

There is one more video for me to look at, but my heart is already racing.

Claire is such a bitch to put me in this situation. Such a genius as well, but *such a bitch.*

When I pull up my call history, I notice that my fingers are trembling.

How can I resist? He's beautiful, intelligent, incredibly funny… If nothing else, I would love to share just one night with him if he'll have me. Men like him don't just grow on trees...

But I'd have to be on TV for us to meet. *Uggh!*

Would it be worth it?

I dial her number and it doesn't even ring once before she picks up.

"And?" she asks.

Her voice is expectant, like she already knows what I'm about to say.

"You suck," I respond.

"So, you'll do it?"

I sigh deeply and pinch the bridge of my nose. I want to meet this man, I do. My heart is racing at the thought.

"Promise you'll cut it if I make a total arse of myself?"

She laughs. "Yes, I promise! I have final say on edits anyway."

I sigh again. "When's this thing happening?"

"Are you free tomorrow? We'd like to wrap up the show quickly."

I can't believe I'm doing this. This entire deal is so far out of my comfort zone, it's not even funny. It's not even that I worry about what people will say, though office gossip will be out of control once it airs… It's basically the cameras. Cameras make me nervous.

Why the hell am I even considering this? Oh yeah, because of *him.*

"Okay. Message me the details," I hear myself say.

Claire starts gushing about how I'm the best and I'm totally saving her ass. She'll owe me forever. I'm not even listening anymore. All I can think about is: what am I going to wear? Will our attraction be mutual?

Am I going to regret my decision?

***

The set is a restaurant in the city. My nerves are out of control as I get off the bus and walk the rest of the way. The uneven pavement is making me feel even more unsteady on my sky high heels.

Really, my knees are the bigger problem, though. They're trembling already, and I haven't even met him yet. Will I even know what to say? I'm crap at dates, especially blind ones. Either it's one word answers, or I'll blurt out the wrong thing at absolutely the wrong time.

The exterior of the restaurant comes into view. I force myself to take a few deep, slow breaths. My forehead is damp and my make-up is threatening to melt off. I rub my clammy hands together in an effort to warm up.

"You've got this, woman! He's probably just as nervous as you are!"

I'm not convincing enough, though, because I'm about ready to pass out.

A few passers-by give me a weird look. I wave them

off. "Don't worry about me, I'm only talking to myself!"

They quickly move away, like I'm some lunatic to be shunned.

I probably am, for even considering this crazy idea.

Another deep breath later, I give myself a quick once-over in one of the shop windows. I look hot, though. I mean… The dress I've picked for tonight is form-fitting but not too slutty. There's enough cleavage to give him something to look at, but I don't think I come off like a whore.

And my arse does look great in these heels.

I may not be a model, but I'm not half bad, if I say so myself. Hopefully he agrees.

After one final pep-talk I head for the doors, open them, and walk in with my head held high.

It's not quite what I expected. The doors don't lead to the bar I saw in the videos at all. Instead there's a lobby which is absolutely buzzing with activity.

Duh, of course. It's a set, after all; it's going to be a bit staged. Claire spots me and comes rushing over.

"Alison. So glad you could make it!"

I force a smile. "You didn't leave me much choice."

She hugs me and takes a step back. "Make-up!" She calls out and snaps her fingers.

A girl carrying a big black bag comes running and starts adjusting my hair, and applies a bit of powder to my face. I *knew* I was getting damp and whatever she's doing, it's making me feel even more clammy.

"Okay, so here's what's going to happen," Claire says.

I'm only half listening, because I'm scanning the filled lobby looking for the man from the videos. He *is* here, isn't he? She better not have tricked me!

"Liam is already inside, at the bar. We've done a few takes of his arrival already. Yours will be one take only, to keep things as natural and genuine as possible. Remember that this is supposed to be a totally *blind* date. You *don't know anything about who you're meeting!* Give the game away and I get into huge trouble."

"Okay…" My mind is racing. Pretend not to know anything about him. Got it.

"Just be yourself. You will have seen from the clips he's a sarcastic bastard just like you. I think you'll get along great."

"Right…" I try not to be offended at the sarcastic bastard comment.

"And I mean… he's your type, right?" Claire asks.

I nod absentmindedly. "Yeah, he's cute."

"I knew it! Awesome. Go break a leg."

"I hope not," I remark dryly, while taking a few unsteady steps towards the door Claire is pointing at.

"Just ignore the cameras. You'll be perfect," she calls after me.

Ignore the cameras. If only things were that simple.

I take one final breath and push the door open. It gives way very easily, and finally I see the scene I had expected to find all along.

He's there. *Liam,* she said. But I'm not supposed to know his name yet. I can vaguely see the bartender as well, but my sole focus is on *him.*

Jesus, he's even more imposing in person. He looks so tall even while sitting down. His physique dwarfs everything around him. From the bar, to the stools lined up in front of it. *Everything.* I feel tiny and insignificant in comparison, because I am.

I try not to let it show and put on my most genuine smile as I walk faux-confidently in his direction.

"Hi!" I say.

He gets up and towers over me. Our eyes meet and I'm breathless. Still, I try to maintain my smile through the relentless hammering of my heart.

"Hi, I'm Liam. Nice to meet you," he says.

His voice. It's rich and deep, and a million times more seductive than what I heard on the video. I have absolutely no trouble at all reacting genuinely to his presence. This isn't what I expected. It's better.

"Alison."

I look down at his hand, stretched out in my direction, but decide to go for a little side-hug instead. There's something about him that draws me in. Hopefully my choice of greeting lets him know I'm interested already.

He reciprocates awkwardly, with his hand brushing the bare skin on my shoulders, leaving goosebumps in his wake.

I inhale and catch a bit of his scent when our quick greeting is interrupted much too soon by his withdrawal. It's as rich and seductive as his voice. To say that I'm still attracted to him would be the understatement of the century.

"Lovely place, this," I remark. "Do you come here often?"

What a stupid attempt of a joke.

He nods briefly. Apparently he thinks it was a dumb remark too, because he's no longer looking at me.

"That's funny," he lies.

I bite my bottom lip. He sits back down and picks up his drink to take a sip. Looks like whiskey of some sort.

"Sooo, what's good here," I wonder aloud, while scanning the bottles behind the bar.

The bartender gives me a quick smile and leans forward while waiting for my order.

"I'll have whatever he's having," I say.

That earns me a suspicious side-eye from Liam.

"Hope you like single malt," he remarks.

Frankly, I don't much care. First of all, I want to learn what *he* likes, secondly, I just can't think of anything to order. And I desperately need to calm the fuck down already.

The barkeep prepares my drink, puts it down on a napkin and slides it over to me.

"Cheers," I say, raising my glass in Liam's direction.

He mirrors my gesture, and lets his gaze pause on me for a moment. I hope he likes what he sees, but his expression could not be more guarded.

I smile at him and take my first sip.

"Oh, this is the good stuff," I say. "Peaty."

He nods, but there isn't a hint of a smile to be seen. I remember his earlier disappointments, the recordings of which Claire had sent to me, which I've accidentally reminded him of already too. It's no wonder he's shut down. You can only put yourself out there so many times before it gets too painful.

Still, if this is how tonight is going to be, it won't be the *win* Claire had hoped for.

Or he doesn't like me. That's also a possibility.

Maybe I'm just not his type?

"Would you two like to come through?" One of the suited and booted waiters approaches us and guides us through to an empty square table. We carry our drinks over and place them down at the two place settings which have already been laid out for us.

There are four cameras set up all around the table, to catch all the angles. I hate it; how self-conscious all of this makes me feel. And that's on top of the distinct coldness I'm feeling from him.

The waiter first helps me get seated by pushing my chair in, and then does the same for him.

Now that we're opposite one another, I have literally nowhere else to look but at him. I try to maintain eye contact, but his eyes keep darting around the place settings, my face, my hair, somewhere in the distance…

I want to say something clever, something funny to break the ice, but the words evade me. I'm so taken in by his imposing physique that my mind has gone absolutely blank.

"You're really tall," I remark. *Duh.*

He glances at me briefly. "Six-four."

"Nice!" I say. "Hope you don't mind dating someone much shorter."

He shrugs.

"I mean, I'm five-six, so I'm not *short,* short, but it's a bit of a contrast still..."

From the corner of my eye, I see Claire talking to a couple of other girls with headsets on. Then she looks at me and gestures at me to keep talking.

Someone has to, because he might as well be mute. Remembering the videos I'd seen, I decide to pick a relatively easy topic of conversation.

"Tell me a bit about yourself. What are your passions? What do you like to do in your spare time?" I ask.

I could have asked about his job, but really, who cares? Work talk doesn't get most people excited. I want to see the side of him I saw in the videos. Not this suspicious shell of a person. More than anything, I want an opening to maybe try and flirt. Although I'm not very good at that sort of thing.

"The usual. Music, films, TV."

"What's the last TV show you saw and liked?" I ask.

Finally, I see a flicker of something in him. A hint of a change. He shifts in his seat. "This twist on the superhero genre. The Boys. You may not have seen it."

I lean forward. "Are you kidding, I loved it! Binge watched it last weekend!"

For a change, I'm not even lying.

He seems to pick up on my excitement and stares at me. "Really!"

"Karl Urban was hilarious in it."

"His accent was shit." He glances at the cameras and

catches himself. "Sorry."

"Yeah, but his lines were the best," I say with a wide grin. "That scene at the religious festival thing when he started ranting at the priest. Damn!"

"Agreed." He runs his hand across his neatly trimmed beard and smiles briefly. God, I wish I could reach out and touch it too. "So, you like superheroes, huh?"

I shrug. "I'll watch anything, really. As long as it's violent."

He nods slowly. "No romantic comedies and that sort of stuff?"

I make a face. "Not unless I'm PMS-ing."

He snorts and tries to hide his amusement by taking a sip of Scotch.

In the background I see Claire face-palming herself. *Fuck you, and your sarcastic bastard remark earlier.*

Finally, we're getting somewhere. He's visibly relaxing, and I'm starting to feel more in my element, despite the audience of cameras and producers and random other people that continues to surround us.

A waiter arrives to take our order. I just pick the first thing from the menu that looks halfway edible and focus on Liam again. He's equally disinterested, and keeps glancing up at me instead.

Does he like what he sees? Finally, he also decides on his order.

"This is awkward, isn't it?" I ask, as the waiter leaves us again. "First dates are always so… Ugh!"

He smiles briefly and nods. "Yeah, I guess so."

"I like second dates much better. Everything is still new. The mystery is still there, but at least you know enough about the other person already to be sure whether you like them."

We stare at each other for a few seconds. There are so many questions in his eyes, and yet he's not asking a single one of the pertinent ones.

"The trick is getting to that second date, though," he remarks dryly at last.

There it is. The real him. A cynic at heart, who has been burned one too many times.

"True, that. If I had my pick of a superpower, perhaps that would be the one to go for. Guaranteed second dates at will. That would take a lot of the anxiety out of it all."

Again, those eyes are on me. Full of curiosity and wonder. If I'm not careful, I'll end up way too invested in this date, way too soon. So far he hasn't given me any clues as to whether he likes me back or not.

My eyes are drawn to the rest of him. I'd seen plenty on my way in, but there's just so much to look at that I find it hard not to stare. He really is a vision of perfection. His body promises a tactile overload a smaller lover cannot provide. If he knew just how much I crave his touch already… Thankfully he isn't a mind reader or tonight might get even more awkward.

"Tell me about your musical tastes," I say. "Personally, I'm more of an alternative sort of person. The louder the guitars, the better."

"Are you, now?" He leans back and squints.

"Funny."

I knew from the videos Claire had sent that there would be quite an overlap in our tastes. What I had planned to present as a happy coincidence, he is now reacting to with suspicion. It wasn't my intention to put him off.

"What's funny?" I ask, though I'm pretty sure I don't want to hear the answer to that question.

"Just. You seem to know exactly what to say."

I bite my bottom lip. "I'm just being honest. Isn't that the dating advice that's given normally? Be yourself."

"Yeah… Or…"

I raise my eyebrows and wait for his inevitable conclusion. This date is definitely taking a turn for the worse. I glance over at Claire, who is slowly shaking her head. I guess I laid it on too thick.

A man like him, after the shit experiences he's been through shooting this idiotic TV show, is bound to be suspicious. She *had* asked me for help, but I wasn't doing this for her.

My turning up and playing along with this dumb plan was an entirely selfish move. All these nerves, all this anticipation. It wasn't to save Claire's job. It was because even during that first video clip of him I was hopelessly lost. Invested. Enchanted.

He pushes his chair back and gets up.

"You can cut now," he grumbles and walks away, leaving me, the crew, and the waiter who is bringing our starters absolutely stunned. "Nice try. But I think I'm done with this whole charade."

"What the actual fuck?" I blurt out and watch while he leaves me at the table.

Claire rushes over and tries to intercept Liam, but he's having none of it and brushes her off. Then she approaches me with a scowl on her face.

"Dude. What the hell did you say to him?" she asks.

"We were having a nice chat, I thought. Listen to the recordings if you don't believe me. I guess he's a bit paranoid, huh?"

"Keep your voice down." She snaps her fingers again, and gestures at one of the headset girls to go after Liam, who's making a beeline for the men's room.

"Look, You know me. I wouldn't have come if I didn't want to at least give it a good try," I say.

"Yeah, well. Good intentions aren't going to fix this. He's walked off and next I'm going to get it from the bosses."

I take a deep breath and watch him disappear behind the heavy wooden door. "I really do think he's cute."

That's when anger hits. Not only did I do something I *really* didn't want to, I did it for him more than for Claire. And now he's making a scene and stomping off like a diva, rather than giving this thing a chance. Don't I deserve better than *that* at least? I'm going to make him hear my side of things, if it's the last thing I ever say to him.

I get up and join the headset girl who is uncomfortably shuffling from foot to foot outside the men's room.

"He doesn't want anyone to go in," she warns me. "I already got it from him when I knocked."

"Well, tough shit," I say.

I push the door open and am met with immediate protests.

"What did I say? Will you people just leave me the hell alone already!" Liam shouts.

"You don't talk to me like that until I've said my piece," I counter.

Like an amazonian warrior, I square off against him with hands on my hips while the bathroom door slowly closes behind me.

There's no one else inside but Liam, who had retreated to the furthest washbasin near the urinals. Good. The last thing we need is an audience.

He looks up, half surprised, half angry.

"*Alison*. If that's even your name."

I glare at him. "That *is* my name. Why wouldn't it be?"

"Oh, I dunno. Because you're an actress hired by that Claire woman? Because there's no way this was going to work out otherwise, and she needed to make a feel-good episode to finish off her show?"

"Wait, so you think- and I want you to think really carefully before you respond to this question-" I take a deep breath, savouring my anger while it gives me courage. "*You* think I'm some bimbo who got paid to go on this date today? Actress sounds a lot nicer, but what you're really saying is 'escort', aren't you? Because that's what you call women who go on dates for money."

He takes a step back and opens his mouth, only to close it again. "That's not… Ok, I can see how it sounds bad when you put it that way."

"Let me tell you something, mister." I step up to him and poke him in the chest with my index finger. The fact that the top of my head only measures halfway up his chest doesn't put me off in the slightest. I'm furious.

"If this is how you react to every woman who's trying to make a pass at you, then it's no wonder your previous dates haven't panned out."

I know I'm being unfair, but hell… So is he.

"What the fuck are you talking about?" he sounds more shocked than defensive now.

"Seeing as the cat is already half out of the bag, I might as well tell you everything. What have we got to lose?"

"Okay…"

"Claire is a friend of mine," I say.

"I knew it!" he exclaims.

"You don't know shit." I fold my arms and continue to stare him down. "I'm not a fucking charity, okay? Neither am I getting paid a penny for this. Let me finish first before making your judgements."

"Fine. *Please*, carry on." The sarcasm is dripping off his voice. I kinda like it.

"She told me about you and asked if I wanted to go on this date. I said yes. Not as a favour to her, but because I genuinely wanted to."

"And why would you do that, if not as a favour?"

"Because I wanted to meet you. Thought you were

cute," I say with a shrug.

My heart is racing so hard I can feel it in my throat. Although I'm still angry, those same old nerves have made a comeback.

"I've been called a lot of things in my life, but cute isn't one of them."

I flip my hair back. "Whatever."

"Since you admit that you've been coached, how am I supposed to believe anything you say now?"

I walk up to him and stop only when we're inches apart. His cologne hits me as hard as it did when we had our first weird side-hug at the bar. Still, I try to maintain my composure.

"You can believe whatever you want, but I haven't lied about anything. Claire thought that I might like you, so she called me. That's all there is to it."

"Claire thought… Right. *Sure!*"

"And I haven't been *coached,* as you call it." My bottom lip is trembling ever so slightly. I wonder if it's noticeable. A crack in my otherwise confident veneer.

"Okay, but?" he asks.

We're so close. It would be so easy to do something stupid. To get ahead of myself and let instinct take over. Does it matter if Claire's a friend, as long as we click somehow? Why is he being so difficult about the whole thing?

"But…" My voice trails off. The pained look in his eyes drives me wild. "Well I guess it's a moot point now, since things have already gone to shit."

"This stupid show must mean a lot to you guys,

seeing as you're trying so hard to convince me of something I know is utter bullshit," he argues.

"I couldn't give a fuck about the show."

"You certainly were very keen to be on TV, though."

Again, I'm enraged. He has no idea. "*Keen?* The moment I saw all the cameras I almost shit myself."

A flutter of a smile plays on his lips. "Don't you have a way with words?"

I shrug. "I'm only telling it as it is."

"Then why do it?" he asks.

I roll my eyes. Either he's being thick on purpose or he's enjoying teasing every last bit of information out of me.

"Claire *may* have sent me a few videos, okay? From your previous shoots. I really am not supposed to tell anyone because her job hangs in the balance, but that's how it happened."

"And you *still* agreed to come on?" he asks.

His demeanour changes again. Gone is the little smile. His combative stance is replaced by surprise.

"Liam. Initially I'd told her 'no'. I agreed *because* of the videos. I liked what I saw."

"You're so full of shit." He shakes his head and turns away from me toward the large mirror behind the washbasins.

I frown and shake my head. "You asked. I answered. Now what? Are you going to go out there and get Claire fired, or can we get past this? I thought we were getting along initially, 'til you got all pissed off and fled."

His head snaps back in my direction. "I didn't flee!"

I cock my head to the side and give him a knowing look. "Then what do you call storming off like a diva after shouting at everyone?"

"I just don't enjoy being fucked with. I came on this show, because…"

"Yeah, why, exactly?" I demand. "Why did *you* come on the show?"

"Because I thought maybe something good would come out of it. I certainly wasn't having any luck with internet dating and all the rest of it. The pitch sounded promising; there'd be a team looking for proper matches based on I don't know how many factors… But, I should have known that it's all fake. Reality TV truly is a load of crap."

"I could have told you that reality TV is bullshit from the start. And I've never even been on a set before today. If only we had met without these bloody cameras, things might have turned out differently."

"If we had met anywhere else, you wouldn't have given me a second of your attention.."

I scoff. "Right. If you'd acted equally dickish as right now, then I certainly wouldn't have."

He turns to me again with fire in his eyes. "Okay, I'm being a dick, is that it? Fine. You saw some videos, yeah? Did you see what happened during the other so-called dates? With what Claire claimed were carefully vetted candidates."

I avert my gaze, remembering the intensely awkward scenes I'd seen only yesterday.

"Exactly," he says. "Then you might forgive me for

being a little skeptical."

I take a deep breath. "Okay, that's fair. But that has nothing to do with me. It's not fair that I should have to pay the price for what happened previously. As I see it, I might have turned out to be the most vetted candidate so far. Being Claire's personal pick and all."

"Right, so you waltzed in here, pretended to be all interested and stuff, and-"

"I wasn't pretending, but yeah, carry on. Dig yourself in deeper, why don't you?"

His face is turning a darker shade of crimson and he takes a deep breath, then presses his lips together and just stares at me. It strikes me that actually, he's even cuter when he's angry.

"Why are you even still arguing with me?" he asks after a long pause. "Why did *you* come here tonight?"

"Because it's a hell of a lot more interesting than falling asleep in front of the TV," I say.

"What are you getting out of this? If you're not getting paid, then what is it? A job offer? Something?"

"That's ridiculous. I already have a job, thank you very much! What I've seen here tonight has made me appreciate its boring and non-glamorous nature even more."

"What, then?"

It's time I got my message across a bit more firmly. Clearly my words are falling on deaf ears so far. "Well, I thought I'd have a nice evening, meet an interesting man, see where it leads - perhaps a one night stand, perhaps more..."

"Wait, *what?*"

I look up at him and bat my eyes. "What?"

"Did you seriously just say-"

"What did I say? 'One night stand'?" I ask, clearly enunciating the words.

"Are you sure Claire sent you *my* videos? What part of those made you think about sex, exactly?"

Aaand he's taken the bait. Time to reel him in.

I shrug. "I thought you came across as intelligent, and really funny. A good sense of humour is an aphrodisiac, you know? Then, physically-"

"Yeah, let's talk about that. *Physically.*"

"Well physically it's an obvious yes from my side. I think you're hot. What else is there to think about?"

"Now I'm certain you're taking the piss," he complains.

"You've got issues, you know that," I remark.

"I do, yeah. But I'm starting to think that perhaps you have bigger issues. Like, how's your eyesight?"

"Wow, okay. That's not nice." I shake my head. "As I said, if only you weren't acting like a total prick right now, things might have turned out differently."

I'm saying that. And I should believe it. But there's something about his hostility which only makes me want him more. Maybe it's true what they say. Women really do like men who treat them like dirt.

I stare him down, and he stares back. The look in his eyes softens, and my heart responds.

"You're right," he says finally. "That wasn't nice. I apologise."

"Thank you. Apology accepted."

We're both still staring, but not angrily anymore. That hint of vulnerability I saw in his videos, it's made a comeback. I want to claim it for myself.

"Now what?" he asks.

I should punish him some more, but I can't bear the look in his eyes.

"I'm still up for it, if you are," I say in a softer tone.

"Up for what, exactly?" he asks. There is a rawness in his voice that makes me cream myself. It's so true what they say: men can't catch subtle cues. They need to be hit over the head with it. Although this private conversation wasn't the most pleasant part of the date, it was probably necessary to get all the ugliness out into the open.

I shrug, but maintain eye contact. "For… whatever."

"I…" he presses his lips together. Those full, sensual lips that look like they were made to be kissed.

"How about this? Why don't you figure out what it is you want out of this, exactly? I told you I'm attracted to you already. Nothing has changed there, and you *did* apologise, which I accepted... Now, you tell me."

"Tell you what?" he asks.

He glances downward at my cleavage, as if I wouldn't notice. Then, he looks up at my face again.

"Tell me if you feel the same way," I say.

He exhales loudly and shrugs. "Well, uhh, you're a beautiful girl."

I smile briefly, trying to play it cool. "I believe the socially acceptable term nowadays is 'woman'."

"Right. A beautiful woman."

It's a start.

"Thanks. Am I your type, though?" I ask. "If you're not feeling it, then there's no point in carrying on. So… Are you feeling it?"

My heart is racing, and every fiber in my body is screaming at me to run and hide. But I don't. Instead, I inch forward and get even closer to him. Our bodies are almost touching and it's threatening to drive me crazy.

"I was so weirded out about the whole circus out there, I haven't even thought about any of that," he confesses.

Not what I wanted to hear. And yet, his body language tells me that perhaps he does have a few more intimate thoughts. His shoulders are hanging low, his eyes seem unwilling to focus on either my eyes or any other part of my anatomy and keep darting back and forth. He's sweating, and his hands are unable to keep still. I'm making him nervous and I love it.

This mountain of a man must be infinitely stronger than I am. And yet it looks like I've got him helplessly cornered. The tables have turned; his nerves give me strength.

"Then why don't you figure it out right now?" I ask sweetly.

"How?"

"Make your move, big man. See what happens. If it feels right?" I can't believe I'm hearing myself. My earlier anger has given me a kind of courage I've never felt before. If he doesn't bite, I'll be heartbroken.

He takes a deep breath and just stares at me. The air between us is electric, and yet he's frozen in place for an endless number of seconds. Then he leans down, gently places his hand on my shoulder and coaxes me toward him.

His lips softly brush mine. Short breaths tickle my face. I swoon and almost lose my balance.

I steady myself with both hands against his chest, then let one hand travel upward and guide his face down further.

"Now you've gone and made my knees weak," I whisper.

Our lips finally fuse, my heart rejoices. Every one of my feelings and urges is confirmed. He's perfectly breathless, as am I. Our tongues seek out one another, and engage in a feverish dance of passion. I raise myself up with both my arms wrapped around his neck. He picks me up by the hips and effortlessly lifts me up just high enough to set me onto the counter space next to the washbasin. We never stop kissing throughout.

I spread my legs as wide as they'll go in this dress, allowing him to position himself closer to me. He can't resist the invitation.

He's so huge, his body overwhelms me. Although I've had larger lovers before, they were nothing compared to him. His kisses already tell me he's going to be amazing in bed. Attentive, enthusiastic, with bucket loads of raw talent to satisfy my every need.

His fingers thread through my hair, his other hand finds its way around my waist, pulling me tightly against him. I'm completely taken over by him. He owns me already, and he doesn't even realise it.

Then, much too soon, he withdraws and opens his eyes to look at me. His cheeks are flush, his lips slightly parted and his eyes clouded with desire.

"Are you feeling it yet?" I whisper. "Because I am."

The intense stare he's giving me tells me all I need to know.

"You're... " he starts, then just exhales sharply.

I lean in again and gently pluck at his bottom lip with my teeth. God, I could eat him up. Tonight has been really intense already, so confusing and infuriating at the start. And yet, this moment we're sharing in the men's bathroom is utterly perfect.

"Why would a girl- sorry, a woman like you…"

I blink innocently. It's obvious what he wants to know. I'm not sure my answer will satisfy him.

"Why me?" he says.

I don't immediately answer, I just tug at him to get closer again and start kissing and nibbling his neck. His scent overwhelms. I wonder what cologne he's wearing, because I'm going to need to buy a bottle just to relive the memory of this moment when I'm alone. Over and over again.

"I think you're sexy, Liam. It's why I wanted to meet you."

He groans when I sink my teeth into him just a little harder.

"I've never felt this way," he whispers.

That's a crying shame, even if I could say the same.

Our reconciliation has been spectacular, perhaps more so because of all the doubts and arguments we had to get out of the way first. Or maybe it's just the effect he's had on me from the start.

"Maybe… You know, if you're okay with it… We could get this stupid shoot out of the way and be alone somewhere other than the men's room?" I suggest. "I mean, this is nice and all, but it's a bit trashy. It's not exactly my scene."

"I can't go out there. Not now," he says.

His tone is almost apologetic, if it wasn't so laden with emotion of another type.

I glance downwards, but his large physique doesn't give me a clear view of his crotch. Still, I can guess what he means. My heart surges with excitement. I've got him exactly where I want him; struggling for control.

"Are you hard for me, Liam?" I ask, while looking at his face through my lashes.

His expression turns bashful.

"It's okay," I whisper. "I'm going to take that as a compliment."

His huge belly, pressing up into me barely gives me enough room, but I slip off the counter regardless. He towers over me again, his arms hanging helplessly by his sides.

"I'm going to need a moment alone," he says.

I know exactly what he needs, even if he's too shy to say so himself.

I bite my lip and look up at him. "Are you sure that's what you want? *Alone?*"

He's avoiding eye contact. I can tell he's conflicted. Probably part of him is embarrassed to even admit this to me. I wonder if I can push my luck just a little bit further.

"Or would you like a hand with that… issue…?" I lick my lips, and glance up at him expectantly.

"Jesus. Uhh…"

"I don't mean to intrude, but… Maybe I could be of assistance, you know?" I continue to tease.

"I couldn't possibly ask you to. I mean… We've only just met." When he looks into my eyes, he goes quiet again.

"You're not asking, I'm offering," I remind him.

He's frozen in place when I run my hands over his chest, momentarily rest them on top of his humongous belly, before heading way down past the various ripples and folds of his endless torso. There, just where the overhang of the largest part of his belly ends, I pause.

"Why are you doing this?" he mumbles, through strained breaths.

"Because I want you."

"It's just… This is all so unexpected."

"May I?" I gently prod and explore his underbelly, but make sure not to go too far down without his reassurance.

My chest is tight, my heart racing.

His reluctance is just an act; a thin veil covering countless unspoken desires. I can see it in his eyes. In his impatiently shallow breaths.

"Uhhh." He shrugs, but his eyes are wide now. That

deer-in-headlights look again. "I guess."

"I just want to make you feel good," I say, and reach deeper between his thighs until I find something firm hiding underneath the thick layers of fat.

He shudders at my touch.

"You're going to have to help me out," I whisper. "Turn around and lean against the counter."

He nods and shuffles into position, with both his hands holding on to the edge of the marble until his knuckles show white.

This is all wrong, and yet feels so right. I'm supposed to play hard to get; to make him work for it. But my patience has worn thin.

I fight with the button and zip of his jeans, until they give way. I wish I could see him fully naked. To discover all the joys as yet hidden underneath these clothes. But this isn't the time or place. I'll have to earn the privilege of seeing him in his full glory another time. And that's exactly what I'm aiming for now. To work for his approval.

I explore him by touch. The soft flesh of his thick thighs, the smattering of hair on his lower belly, and finally, upon slipping my hand into his briefs, I find his hard cock.

"Look at you, you're so hard and thick," I coo and wrap my fingers around his solid length.

"Oh, God," he gasps.

"Show me how you like it," I whisper.

He doesn't stir. In fact he seems to freeze up more when I start slowly pumping his cock, and really making an effort to dig in to reach the base of his shaft which remains obscured by luscious fat.

I look up at him, and see his zen-like expression. Eyes closed, features relaxed, save for that one deep crease between his eyebrows. His breaths have sped up further, causing his whole body to shiver and jiggle along.

"May I taste you?" I ask.

His eyes snap open in shock.

"That's what you want? *Really?*" he protests in between quick gasps.

I stand on tiptoes and plant a quick kiss on his lips. "If you'll let me."

He's so far gone, I'm certain he's not going to last. His dick is growing even prouder in my hand. If I want a taste, I'm going to make it quick before it's too late.

"Okay, sure…" he moans.

I get down on one knee, while keeping my other foot planted securely on the ground for stability.

"Give me some room, okay?" I ask.

He reluctantly lets go of the counter, and lifts his large belly up just enough to allow me access.

He has a beautiful cock. Thick and lush, like the rest of him. And it's really long as well, though most of it is swallowed up by his luxurious body at this angle.

I hold onto it firmly, trying my best to force its shroud of fat out of the way, and go in for my first taste.

He shudders into my face. Nose, eyes, forehead, everything gets pressed deeply into his flesh.

His scent overpowers me, in a good way.

He tastes salty, yet fresh, and oh so manly. He's a god.

His hand finds the back of my head, but he doesn't push or force my rhythm, instead he lets me do my own thing.

I do my best to perform for him. To suck him as deeply and hard as I can, while building up a faster and faster pace. His hips buck uncontrollably, I steady myself with one hand against his thigh and carry on.

Before long, his moans turn into louder, more animalistic groans. His breathing is out of control and his hand twitches and spasms in my hair. His whole body starts to lose control, one limb and muscle group at a time, until he's rigid, panting, and covered in a thin layer of sweat.

"I'm going to-" He doesn't finish his sentence. It's unnecessary anyway, because I already know.

His cock convulses, and shoots its load deep into my throat. I swallow everything, then continue to suck him slowly and deeply, milking every last drop of cum out of him. His hand slides off my head and rests on the counter again.

While he's busy catching his breath, I get myself up and admire my handiwork. He's done for. Conquered.

He's completely and utterly mine.

I tug at his jeans, aiming to hitch them back up, but am unsuccessful until he startles into action and helps me out. While I watch him do-up his button with trembling fingers, a knock on the door interrupts us.

"Don't come in, we'll be right out!" he shouts, but

the door has already opened about half.

I catch a glimpse of Claire's questioning face on the other side.

I'm going to hear about this later, but I'm not even remotely embarrassed. What does she care, as long as she gets what she wants, right?

"God, these people are tenacious!" Liam complains.

I suppress a grin and point at his face. "You've got a bit of lipstick on you."

He leans towards the mirror and wipes it off, meanwhile I do the same to fix my hair and apply a fresh coat to my lips.

"Let's get this bullshit over with, what do you say?" I suggest. "The night has only just begun."

He looks at me awkwardly. "Yeah, alright."

I gesture at him to leave first, and can't resist the urge to give him a little smack on the ass. He freezes, while I catch up.

"By the way, you're returning the favour afterwards," I whisper. "I'm soaking wet just for you."

His expression is everything. I've won.

I pass him by with a spring in my step and emerge from the bathroom first.

Claire's waiting outside with her arms folded and a disapproving scowl on her face.

"Yeah, so, we talked it out. We can carry on with the shoot now." I try to sound nonchalant, but I'm not sure it's working.

She slowly shakes her head. "Alison… Like… Wow."

It's probably not a compliment, and yet…

"You're getting what you want, aren't you?" I whisper. "Don't ruin it."

That reminder makes her regain her composure.

"Alright, guys. Positions! Please, take a seat and redo the conversation from earlier. Getting to know one-another."

I smile and nod. Liam joins me at the table and takes a seat. His eyes never waver. He's staring uncontrollably.

Good. Perhaps now we'll have that on-screen chemistry I was hoping for all along.

I take a deep breath and smile. He smiles back at me. It makes my heart jump.

"Tell me about yourself, Liam. What are you passionate about?" I start again.

His answers are similar, but this time, reveal more of his real self. I respond in kind.

The starters arrive again, and we offer each other bites to taste. *So* romantic. Conversation flows freely, until I'm ready to ignore the cameras, the people, even Claire.

We get comfortable. We share some banter, some jokes, and plenty of innuendo. By the end of it, he holds my hand across the table.

This was how this was meant to go from the start. How I had envisioned it in my best case scenario.

Time absolutely flies, and before we know it we've made it through our entrees and dessert, and it's time for the next phase of the show.

He steals awkward glances at me while we walk

towards another part of the set. The sofa with the show's logo written across the wall behind us. 'Sealed with a kiss'.

I know what's coming, and I'm excited about it already. Whatever Claire expected out of tonight, it no longer matters, because I already know what I'm going to do. What *I* want.

Liam, meanwhile, is looking uncomfortable again.

"Relax, will you," I whisper.

He leans over, while scanning the buzz of activity around us. Cameramen setting up their equipment all around, Claire and the other producers running around, doing who knows what.

"I'm sorry, this bit is cringeworthy."

"Why?" I play dumb.

"Well, I mean… All these people, and then a TV audience. It's tacky."

I turn to face him. "Do you care that people are watching?" I ask.

He averts his gaze and scans the room again. "Umm, I dunno."

"Do you think it's wrong to show affection in public?" I continue.

He shrugs. "I don't have a problem with that, but I don't want to embarrass you."

I smile and shake my head. "You *are* cute, you know that? Don't worry about me."

He's about to protest, when the room goes silent and I only hear Claire's last instruction. "Let's roll!"

She sits down on a folding chair in front of us and

starts the obligatory conversation. Would we like to see each other again? First she asks Liam, who obviously says yes, with a nervous smile playing on his lips. All the while, he's stealing glances at me.

I wonder if he's replaying everything that happened in the bathroom earlier?

Then she turns to me and asks me the same. Do I want to seal it with a kiss?

I glance over at Liam. He's fidgeting and avoids the sight of me now. This scenario obviously brings back bad memories. Perhaps I can override them all with another good one instead.

I scoot closer to him and slip my hand around the back of his neck. He stops looking around at everyone and everything, and only has eyes for me now.

I could lose myself in his gaze.

He leans down, just slightly. I feel the tension grow, just like it had done earlier, before our first kiss. Oh, how I'd love to tease out this moment. I glance at his lips which continue to tempt me. And then up at his eyes again, which express a thousand emotions, hopes and dreams, mirroring my own.

"I really like you, Liam. I want to see more of you." I hope he really hears me, subtext and all.

He holds his breath. His eyes glaze over. He's so mine, all I have to do is claim him again.

I lean in, as does he. He gives me a sweet peck on the lips. So short, so unsatisfying. I tug at his neck again, he yields fully and wraps his arms around me, and we kiss like our lives depend on it.

Slowly, gently, deeply. It's perfectly heart wrenching and seductive at once. My cunt was already slick before, but I'm really dripping for him now. It occurs to me that my mouth probably still tastes of dick, which makes this make out session all the hotter.

"I want you," I whisper against his lips, just low enough that the microphones should not be able to pick it up.

He doesn't say anything, just holds me more firmly and kisses me again. This goes on for a minute, maybe two, until we become aware of our surroundings again and break away.

"Cut!" I hear someone shout.

"Thank fuck for that," I whisper.

He frowns.

"Maybe we can finally get out of here now. Skip ahead to that second date, maybe. What do you think?" I ask.

He smiles briefly. "You've moved on from one night stands to second dates now?"

I grin widely. "We'll see about that once you return the favour."

His eyes are fixated on me. Obsessed. I've awoken something in him; a deep, dark urge that refuses to be caged. I cannot wait to find out where his newfound desire will take us.

Claire approaches with a smile on her face. Despite all the earlier confusion, it's obvious she's pleased with the outcome.

"Did you get all that?" I ask sweetly.

"Alison, Liam…" She pauses when she looks at him.

I glance over and find he's still staring at me. It makes me feel warm and fuzzy inside.

"That was great. I think we've got all the footage we need. It's going to be one hell of an episode once it airs."

"Good. Don't make me come back here," I warn.

"I won't. Promise. There's a little paperwork to fill out, Alison. Releases to sign, that sort of thing. After that you'll be all done," she says.

I roll my eyes, but then force myself up off the couch. Liam reluctantly follows my example.

"I guess my stuff is already done, right?" he says.

Claire nods in agreement.

He turns to me. "Okay, so… I'll wait for you in the lobby?"

I give him the thumbs up. "Don't go wandering off anywhere, alright? I'll be out as soon as she lets me go."

Claire sighs and shakes her head as we watch him walk away. I say walk, it's more of a gentle sway. I continue to stare at his arse for a little too long.

"That almost went very wrong," she remarks.

"And yet, it didn't." Things turned out pretty perfect indeed.

"Do I even want to know how exactly you got him to continue the shoot?" she asks.

I lick my lips and smile. "It took a bit of convincing."

"Thank you so much. You really saved me," Claire says. "When he got up and made a scene, I thought that's it. My promotion; done for."

I glance across the busy floor towards the doors behind which he disappeared already. "You're welcome. Though... I didn't do it for you," I muse. "No offense."

"I felt bad for him after the last shoots," Claire says."He's a nice guy, really. He deserves to find someone."

"Are you kidding? He can be quite the animal if given the chance," I quip.

She stares at me with her mouth agape. "You didn't!"

I shrug. I thought her near-interruption in the bathroom had tipped her off already. Apparently not, but the penny has dropped at last. In any case, I'm not even remotely ashamed of what happened. It worked in both our favour.

"No wonder..." Her voice trails off.

"What?"

"I'm saying, it's no wonder he went along with everything after that."

"Hm?"

"Well, considering he's never been with a woman before," Claire remarks.

"He hasn't?" I ask.

"Didn't you see the clips I sent you?" she counters. "The audition interview?"

"You mustn't have sent me everything, because I had no idea. *Shiiiit.* He's a virgin?" I let out a surprised chuckle.

Perhaps I should have guessed from his reactions to

me, but I really didn't even stop to consider it. All through I have been way too focused on my own desires to analyse him all that much.

"He certainly knows how to kiss, though," I observe. "My knees are still jelly."

Claire laughs and pats me on the shoulder. "Okay, if you say so. Let's get through these forms so you two love birds can go, alright?"

I smile and nod while she hands me a stack of documents. I pretend to read them before signing, but all I can think of is Liam. And all the filthy things we're going to get up to once we're alone.

He's not going to be a virgin for much longer, that much is certain!

***

When I leave Claire with the completed release forms, I find Liam waiting in the lobby with his back turned towards me. After everything that's happened tonight already, I wonder what he must be thinking. I hope it's the same as what I've been fantasising about...

"Sooo," I start. "I'm ready."

"Cool." He awkwardly folds his arms in front of his amply padded chest. "Where do you want to go? I mean… I'm assuming the plan is still on."

"Of course we're still on! You're not getting away so easily."

He smiles at me and stuffs his hands into his pockets. It's obvious that he's not quite sure what to do or say. That's fine, though. I understand now.

"Do you want to go to a pub, or something? Or…"

"Or…" I wink at him. "I did say I'd like to spend some time alone with you. I meant it."

"I still don't really get it. Why would you ever want that?"

"What can I say? A girl's got needs."

"I believe the socially acceptable term is 'woman'," he corrects me.

Finally. I'm starting to see more of this part of his personality that had attracted me in the first place. He might be shy and awkward at times, but that's just the nerves dampening his sharp wit.

"You've got me there, yes," I agree.

We start to walk towards the door, even though we haven't decided yet where to go. I can't wait to get away from all these people and their curious stares.

"So, are you like a sapiosexual? Attracted to intellect rather than appearance?" he asks while holding the door for me.

I frown and wait for him to follow him outside. I've heard the term, but that's not me at all. "No, me? I'm pretty much as shallow as they come. Physical attraction is very important to me when it comes to dating. Vital, even."

His expression turns thoughtful again. "Then what on earth are you doing here with me?"

"I already said, didn't I? You're my type."

"You have no idea how hard that is to believe."

"And yet it's true. Over time I've learned that it's counter-productive to pretend otherwise. Or you'll be fooled into thinking I'm a much nicer person than I actually am. I've said it before and I'm saying it again. I'm not a charity. The only person I'm doing a favour for right now is myself," I say.

I slip my hand through the crook of his arm as we head down the street. He instinctively tightens his grip around me and I feel on top of the world.

"You still didn't tell me where you wanted to go," he reminds me.

I smile. Home would be an option. *Home with him.*

But then, a brightly lit building in the distance catches my eye. "How about that hotel?" I say.

It looks nice. Expensive, probably. I've unceremoniously blown him in a restaurant bathroom already, it's only fair his first actual night with a woman takes place in classier surroundings. A night to remember.

He stops in his tracks and follows my gaze. "Are you sure?"

"We've already eaten. And I'm not really in a drinking mood right now." I tug at his arm. "Go on! You only live once, right?"

We share a smile. "Can't argue with that. I just can't help but think that I'm going to wake up from this dream just before we get to the best part."

Such a big, strong man, yet he's carrying so much doubt around with him. What a shame.

I stop and let go of him, only to wrap my arms around his neck. "I have zero intention of letting you fall asleep any time soon. No sleep, hence no waking up."

He looks at me for a moment. Like a much desired present, about to be opened for the very first time. That's enough to make me even more impatient for what is to come. His hands end up on my back, giving me shivers.

"I'm still shocked you kissed me on the couch. In front of all those cameras," he whispers.

"Why wouldn't I? I enjoyed kissing you in the bathroom earlier."

"Don't you worry what people might say?"

I make a face. "I hate people. But I like you; I thought I'd made that clear already."

He smiles briefly, then glances down at my lips. "People are the worst, you're right."

I slip out from his embrace, take his arm and tug at it. "Let's go already. We deserve some privacy after all that nonsense."

With that, I lead the way and he follows half a step behind.

The tastefully decorated lobby of the hotel awaits. We approach one of the two impeccably dressed men staffing the reception desk. Finally, Liam takes the lead and I let him.

It's a male ego thing. The last thing I want is to make him feel inadequate. He's got plenty of hangups about himself as it is.

"We'd like a room, please," he says. "One night."

The receptionist glances at the two of us, smiles politely, then checks his computer. If he's judging us, he's not letting it show.

Meanwhile, I let my eyes wander over the decor of the place. Tasteful. Expensive.

On the counter, I spot a brochure. One of the pictures catches my eye.

"Can we get one of these?" I point to the photograph of the jacuzzi.

Liam, who has already pulled out his credit card gives me an intense stare that sends shivers down my spine yet again.

The receptionist eyes us curiously, as does his colleague.

"It's our anniversary, you know," I lie, with a beaming smile on my face.

I place my hand on Liam's shoulder. God, he's so tall. I want to climb him right now. Of course, I don't. I do stand on tiptoes to get closer to ear height.

"If it's too much, we'll go halves on the room. It's just… it's a bit of a fantasy of mine," I whisper.

Liam swallows hard and turns to face the guy at the desk again. "Is this room available?"

"Yes, of course," the latter furiously types something into his computer.

I'm elated.

Before long, we're presented with a pair of keycards.

"Congratulations on the anniversary! Luggage?" the man asks. Something in this tone tells me it's mostly a rhetorical question.

I just smile sweetly and put my hand through Liam's arm again. "We've got everything we need right here."

Once we reach the lifts, just out of view from

reception, Liam turns to look at me again.

"You're bulletproof, aren't you?"

"What do you mean?" I ask.

"Nothing seems to bother you." He looks at me with hunger in his eyes.

I chuckle and lean against him, enjoying the feeling of his warm body against mine. "I'm going to take that as a compliment."

"It is."

Our lift arrives, the doors slide open. Once inside, I immediately spot the surveillance camera on the ceiling. Still, I put my arms around Liam and draw him in for a passionate kiss. Tonight something just clicked. Cameras might have made me nervous before, but there's no logical reason for that. A lens is just a stand in for a person. And I really don't care who's watching, so what's there to be nervous about?

I have but one solitary aim: to make tonight the best night we've ever had. Nothing else matters.

"I hope you won't be disappointed," Liam whispers against my lips.

His mannerisms and body language betrays a resurgence of nerves. And yet, he continues to take my breath away.

"Never," I say. "I meant what I just said. I have everything I need right here."

He returns my kisses a little harder this time. I let my hands roam over his body more freely. I know what I want: everything.

Despite his earlier release, the tension between us

has grown to dizzying levels again. The night is still young, and there is so much left for us to explore. But the next orgasm has got to be mine or I'll lose my mind.

We barely stop what we're doing to find our way to the room. And when the door unlocks behind me, we've got our hands all over each other again.

We stumble inside, I pull away mid-kiss to dump my purse on the bedside table. He reaches for me, but I am just a little too quick and get away.

"This place is absolutely beautiful. Now this is a second date worth having," I say.

"I see. You enjoy the finer things in life." Liam approaches and glances at the king size bed near the window. "You deserve nothing but the best."

I smile.

The jacuzzi I wanted so badly is situated on a raised plateau within the same room.

As classy as this hotel appears to be, it's obvious what this room was envisioned for. I'm eager to do it justice.

A knock on the door interrupts. While Liam checks who it is, I fiddle with the knobs of the jacuzzi until it starts to fill up. I'm not going to pass by this opportunity. It's a fantasy, after all.

And with him for company… I know the experience will blow my mind.

Liam returns with a bottle of champagne and two glasses. "To help us celebrate our anniversary, apparently."

I smile widely and sit down on the bed, watching

him as he uncorks the bottle. For someone with little dating experience, he's playing his role very well.

"And that's how you do hotels," I brag.

"Don't tell me you've done this before?" he asks, while handing me my glass.

"I used to work in one during the summer before college. Fancy place like this, it's pretty much normal for them to offer some kind of extra if it's a special occasion for the guests."

"Clever."

I raise my glass. "Happy two hour anniversary!"

"Has it been two hours?"

I shrug. "Probably."

We each take a sip. It's perfectly chilled. I cross one leg over the other and really take my time to check him out. That shirt has got to be at least a 5xl. I wonder how heavy he'd feel on top of me.

"I've been wondering," I start.

"Yeah?"

"You *are* okay with all of this, right?" I ask, before taking yet another sip.

"With a one night stand? Yeah… I suppose." He stares at me in that slightly stand-offish fashion of his. Conflicted between wanting to act on his instincts, and not being confident enough to follow through.

I wish he'd sit down next to me already. I wish he'd take me with force.

Patience… I kick my heels off and keep looking up at him.

"It can be just that if you want. Or, it could be *more*."

I take a final sip to finish my glass and get up from the bed again.

The thick carpet feels lush beneath my feet. He puts his own glass down on the sideboard in a hurry, and faces me.

"I'm so short without heels on," I giggle. "You don't mind, do you?"

He inhales sharply when I run my hand up and down the smooth fabric of his shirt.

He might not think he has much *game*, but he did dress up very nicely for our date tonight. Just the right balance between smart and casual. It's nice to know he's made an effort, even though he didn't know who he was meeting or how it would turn out.

I hook my finger into the gap between two buttons and look up at him again.

"How about you take this off for me," I whisper. "Show me what I've been missing all my life."

He inhales sharply when I tug at the bottom of his shirt, releasing it from the firm grasp of his jeans. I take a step back and unzip my dress all the way down.

He fumbles with his buttons, all the while keeping his eyes fixated on me. I wiggle my shoulders and the dress slips down. After snagging briefly on my hips, it finally lands on the floor.

"You're too much," he says. I smile. These looks he's giving me. This is exactly what I've been craving.

He has finally finished with the shirt. I take a step forward again and slip my hands underneath the fabric, allowing myself that all important first touch of bare skin.

"So sexy," I say.

His skin is soft, pillowy almost. He's like a dream wrapped in cotton wool. A giant teddy bear, but with a raging hard-on just for me.

"Take it all off," I urge him.

Despite the trepidation in his eyes, he does what I ask.

What is it about shyness that turns me on so much? Every time he threatens to retreat, I want to drag him back out of his shell further. I need to convince him he no longer has any reason to hide.

"I feel like it's my birthday and Christmas all rolled into one," I say.

He drops the shirt onto the floor beside my dress, and starts on his jeans. It's obvious that he's uncomfortable. For how long has the world tried to convince him that all of this isn't good enough to be on display? It is, though. He's perfect.

I leave a trail of kisses on his chest. Through the soft curls of his hair, over the swollen manboobs, bigger than my own. My hands caress his sides, appreciating, teasing all this excess of flesh that has been reserved for my eyes and my touch only.

"I've never done this before," he confesses.

I already knew, but pretend not to hear.

"I want you so much," I counter.

His eyes burn into me again, the last remnants of doubt are fading. He bites his bottom lip and finally steps out of his jeans.

We're both in our underwear now, but not for long. I reach behind me and unclasp my bra. It falls off me and leaves me utterly free.

His gaze is drawn to my nipples. Hard, painful, desperate for his affection.

He reaches for me, then pauses. I guide his hand into position and take a step closer. Our naked bodies brush against each other. He takes my breath away.

"Perfection," I remark, while reaching for the hard bulge in his drawers.

He instinctively grinds against my hand.

My boob escapes his grasp and instead he runs his hands down my sides and hips, then reaches around and cups my ass. It's a beautiful feeling. He lifts me up against him. I assist with my arms around his neck and kiss him again.

This is going to be my favourite place from now on. Face height, in his firm embrace. His lips on mine, his beard gently scratching at my chin.

This is what a real man feels like. Virile and strong, guided by primal instinct alone.

We stumble backward, he lays me down on the bed and climbs up after me.

He's quite flexible for his size. At first he tries to position himself next to me, but that won't do. I tug at his arm and he partially gets on top. My lips never leave his for more than a second.

His ample belly squashes against me, heightening my need for him a thousandfold.

Kisses, nibbles, licks and moans. All are guided by one shared goal: pleasure.

I let go of him momentarily to wiggle out of my panties, revealing a neatly trimmed triangle of hair.

He's lost all inhibitions. His hands feverishly roam my body. From my shoulder, to my boobs and tummy, until he cups said triangle and gently spreads my lips with his fingers to gain full access to my core.

I let out a loud moan when he curls his hand in between my thighs.

I'm so wet, his finger slides right into me. I meet him with my hips, gyrating upwards into his hand, while my lips seek out more of him to love.

He smells so good. The crook of his neck; that's where I place my first kiss away from his face. He responds by fingering me deeper and nuzzling my hair.

"Yes!" I call out, when he rubs my clit, before plunging two fingers back into my depths.

I reach for his cock, which is hot and solid underneath his fat belly. His fingers pause within me when I grip him hard.

Then, we get into a matching rhythm; grinding and rubbing at each other for maximum pleasure.

It's amazing, and yet inadequate to scratch my itch.

Even with two fingers; thick and strong as they are, my pussy is left wanting. What I really want is in my own hand. This throbbing, fat dick, which feels about ready to explode again.

"I want to feel you inside me," I whisper. He groans through the kisses on my neck. Someone sure loves the dirty talk! I smile and dig my fingernails into his back.

"I don't have a condom." His breath tickles while he speaks.

"I don't mind if you don't," I counter.

This is unusual, of course. I've always been so strict about safe sex. In fact, I've always been quite strict about sex itself. My antics in the restaurant bathroom would have suggested otherwise, but I'm not usually this easy.

It's because I've never fallen in lust this hard. Liam had me before we even met tonight. The videos lay all the groundwork in advance. He only needed to show up to get me *thirsty as fuck*.

Excuses aside, what could be safer? While this is my first lay in months, it's his first, ever, isn't it?

It's surprising just how much that turns me on. I guess that's another part of the shyness fetish I seem to have developed only tonight. Only for him.

"Please, don't torture me any further," I beg. "Will you fuck me?"

He pulls back and looks down at me. I'm sure my hair is a mess and my make-up is a disaster. If he even notices, he doesn't let it show.

"God, I want to. I want nothing more," he confesses.

I spread wider for him, allowing his hand a free reign over my slick cunt.

"Then do it. Make me scream," I say.

He gets up on all fours. The heavy rolls of his belly

shift and sag, hanging down above me like giant meat curtains. It's funny how his giant body moves, but mostly it's unimaginably sexy. Even if I can no longer reach his cock from my position.

I fondle and squeeze his belly instead. He pauses and looks down at where I'm touching him.

"Like… how?" he asks.

When his eyes meet mine again, I see that his self doubt has made a comeback yet again.

No matter what I do, how visibly horny I am for him, he's still battling his inner demons. I intend to kill every last one with my cunt.

"Let's do it on the edge of the bed. You stand there," I suggest, pointing at the nearest spot just off to the side.

He's starting to sweat as he moves off the bed. I shift into position; ass up on one of the plush pillows, with my legs wide as can be and up in the air.

He grabs me mid-thigh, and shuffles in between. I try my best to force my hand underneath his belly and guide his cock towards me, but there's just too much flesh in the way.

"Rest it on top of me," I say, while caressing the fattest part of his belly.

He's embarrassed- his face is reddening- but he doesn't protest.

"Let me feel you," I urge in my most seductive tone. "Come on, baby. I want it all."

He lifts his belly with both his hands and steps up as close as he can get.

"Yes!" I encourage him. "It'll work like this. Trust me."

He reaches for his cock with his right hand and tries to aim.

"Little down," I say.

My eyes snap shut when the head of his cock starts to tease at my entrance.

"Oh thats it! Push!"

He does, and he's in. The sensation of my cunt clenching his dick hits him so hard, he forgets himself and starts thrusting immediately. It burns, but only because I'm gagging for more. The full weight of his massive belly rests on my stomach, and it sends the remainder of my own self control out the window.

Instinct. Here we are.

"Oh yeah," I gasp, in between strokes. "God, this feels so good!"

I open my eyes, as does he. I'm captivated by him. In mere seconds, he's pivoted yet again and lost much of his anxiety.

"You're so tight," he grunts.

"Your cock is so thick," I respond.

He digs his fingers into my thighs and pushes into me more confidently. Though it's a solid bed, it's shuddering with each of his movements. I'm helplessly pinned down in the squishy mattress. Couldn't move an inch even if I wanted to.

But I don't want to either. Everything he's doing is utter perfection.

"Alison," he says.

I reach up and gently squeeze his right nipple. "Mhm?"

His breathing has sped, and little droplets of sweat appear on his brow.

"Alison, you're beautiful."

My lids close involuntarily as pleasure starts to build. "You are. Liam, you're killing me."

He thrusts into me harder. Deeper. His dick is hitting me just right.

"Don't stop," I beg.

He fucks me just a bit faster.

"Just. Don't stop!" I cry out.

I force my eyes open to look at his face. A sense of calm has come over him. Meanwhile I'm climbing my own mountain toward nirvana.

"You're a god, Liam. Make me yours!" I demand.

He digs his fingers into me harder, and carries on. Sweat is starting to run down his face, his chest. He's dripping on me, and I don't even care.

He *is* the best. This moment will have been on his mind; the fodder of many a fantasy, yet forever out of reach. Until tonight. I didn't realise how much I needed this too.

"Oh fuck." I clench my jaw and can do nothing but moan and whimper, as he sends me hurtling over the edge of control. My pussy tightens, my body freezes.

Tears sting the corner of my eyes. My orgasm washes over me and takes my breath away.

He slams into me again and again, his belly jiggles under my fingertips. I need more hands, just to do his body justice. Mine are simply too small to love and appreciate his vast flesh the way he deserves. I'm lost, limp, spent, but he's still working up to his own release.

Just like that, he pauses, buried balls deep in my wet cunt. His hips twitch, as does his fat cock. It squirms deep inside of me. I can almost feel his hot seed being deposited inside my body. Without any condom, I'm marked forever.

I'm his. His first.

I wish he was mine too. Still, the experience has changed me.

He pauses for a while, tries to catch his breath. All the while, he's furiously out of reach.

"Come lie with me," I whisper.

As much as I've tried to play it cool, I crave his closeness now. I'd enticed him with promises of easy sex. No strings attached. Is it ever that simple?

After all the confusion leading up to this point, I need his touch to soothe my body and soul. The ups and downs leading to this glorious crescendo have made me vulnerable.

Or perhaps *he* has.

He straightens himself, his belly lifts off me, allowing me my first deep breath in minutes. Although he hesitates for a moment, he does join me on the bed again. As he lies down beside me, I breathe a sigh of relief.

I marvel at how deeply he sinks into the mattress. I roll towards him, caught in his gravitational pull.

His skin is damp now. Cold with drying sweat. Mine

is too. It doesn't bother me in the least.

It won't be long now, we'll wash it all off in the tub in the corner.

He awkwardly puts his arm around me, and runs his fingers through my hair.

I drape one of my legs over his thigh, marvelling at just how big it is underneath me. How big the rest of him is too.

"You give the best hugs," I sigh.

"Just hugs?" he asks.

I chuckle. His sense of humour has made a comeback. "Ha! You give pretty good dick, too."

He pulls me into his arms just a little tighter.

Every part of his body is soft. Padded. Luxurious. Perfect.

I seek out his lips and kiss him slowly this time. Now that I've had my release, I'm not in a hurry anymore. We have the night at least. And then, we'll see. Hopefully there will be many more nights.

My leg slips up higher, resting just underneath his belly, on his damp crotch. Surprisingly, I find that he hasn't gone fully limp. I'm impressed. Two orgasms in as many hours, and he still has more to give?

"I really do like you," I say. I don't know if I'm telling him, or myself.

"I like you too."

We kiss again. It's more comfortable, more natural each time that we do.

I squeeze his side, then place my hand on his moob just like I'd done earlier during sex. He flinches just a little, as though he's holding his breath.

"You don't mind how I touch you, right?" I ask.

He doesn't immediately answer. His lips pause in front of mine.

"No, I don't mind." His tone doesn't convince me.

I take his bottom lip in between mine and suck on it gently. Such luscious lips. I love it.

"But?" I ask.

"It's all just… very new. It's alien to me."

I sigh and close my eyes, resting my head against his. "Am I making you uncomfortable?"

"I…"

I try to pull back and look at him, but his arm keeps me firmly in place.

The whole room smells of sex. I can clearly identify it through his cologne and the hint of sweat in the air. It's dizzying.

"I worry about getting used to this," he finally says.

His words try to break me, but I have to pry further. Perhaps I gave it away too easily.

"Why wouldn't you want to get used to it?"

"Because I'll never find it again."

I nuzzle the side of his neck until his natural scent overwhelms me. "I know the feeling."

His fingertips caress my naked back and side. Up and down, down and up. It tickles just enough to make me shiver.

"It feels like I'm living a dream; like it isn't real. This sort of thing just doesn't happen to guys like me."

"Evidently, it does."

He shakes his head and guides my face towards his again.

I open my eyes and find that he's already looking at me.

"You know why I reacted so weirdly to you at first?" he asks.

"You thought I was lying. Pretending," I say.

He shakes his head. "I was confused. Frustrated. You looked at me as if you really saw me. Right from the start you made me feel exposed. And yet you didn't judge me. I'd never experienced that before. Didn't know what to do with it."

"Why would I ever judge you?"

"Everyone else does."

I know he's right, no matter how hard I like to rail against that. And I'm not even doing it out of the goodness of my heart. So many people profess body positivity. They speak out against fat shaming, because they're genuine, kind-hearted people and they know it's wrong to judge.

Meanwhile, I'm not nice like that. I didn't have sex with him to make a statement of morality or to be a social justice warrior. I'm just selfish. He'd better not misunderstand.

"I'm not a saint, you know. I've made my own judgements. I'm nothing more than a catcaller in the street, lusting after a stranger. It just so happens that you turn me on."

He smiles and shakes his head again. "You have no idea what you've done for me already."

I lean up and frown. "But I'm doing it for *me*, more than anything! I'm basically using you."

"That's what's so perfect about you. I never expected to become the object of someone's desire."

I want to argue further, to once and for all bury the idea that I'm this kind-hearted person who has done him a favour, but he silences me with a kiss.

"Shush now. Don't ruin the moment," he warns me when he briefly pulls away.

I'm overcome by him again. Enchanted and hopelessly lost. I could stay here forever, in his arms, enjoying the sweet affections of his lips and hands.

Still, I can't fully let it go. When our kisses slow again, I can't help myself and bring it up again.

"You know I'm not the only one, right?" I ask.

He raises an eyebrow.

"There's a whole community out there. Men who like big women. Women who like big men. Etcetera," I say.

He shrugs. "Can't be much of a trend, seeing as you're the only one I've ever come across."

I snuggle against his shoulder and run my fingertips up and down his naked chest. He's so beautiful. I wouldn't change a thing about him.

"That just now, was my first time," he whispers.

His deep baritone makes me feel weak inside. Or perhaps it's the importance of his words.

I snuggle up to him even closer. "I know."

"I'm thirty-six, and yet… That was it."

"You're an excellent lover," I remark. Again, I'm not

even telling him that just to be nice. It's just the truth.

"You don't think I'm a loser?" he asks.

"Not at all," I say. "But what I can't wrap my head around…"

"Yeah?"

"You tell me all this, and yet earlier you seemed more shocked about the on-camera kiss than the blow job in the bathroom. Objectively, I suppose it should have been the other way around?" I bite my bottom lip, suppressing a naughty smile.

He chuckles. "Yeah, when you put it like that, it's weird, isn't it?"

I smile wider and nod.

"I guess… In the bathroom we were completely alone. If you wanted to deny it later, it would almost be like it never happened. But on camera-"

"There's evidence, therefore making it more real?"

"I suppose."

"It's all real to me," I say, leaning in again for yet another kiss. "And I don't care who sees it."

My lips are starting to get raw, but I can't stop going back for more. As long as he'll have me.

Eventually I do retreat, just for a moment. His arm reluctantly releases me as I raise myself up and lean across to reach the bedside table. I grab my phone from my handbag and nestle back into his embrace.

"What do you say we create some more evidence?" I whisper.

He doesn't respond, but the look on his face tells me my suggestion is hitting home.

I turn on the phone in selfie mode.

Locks of damp hair stuck against my forehead. My mascara has started to bleed a little as well. It doesn't bother me, because it doesn't seem to bother him. This is all part of the memory. We didn't just end up here; we worked up this sweat. The moment I'm capturing hasn't been staged.

The journey up to this point is vitally important to both of us. We'll carry these memories with us for the rest of our lives; at least I know I will.

I smile at the camera and capture a shot with my head resting on his shoulder. Then I face him again. He's already looking at me. I can't get enough of these stares.

Admiration. Affection. Obsession.

Everything I feel in my heart; I see the same and more in his eyes.

I reach for his cheek with my other hand and kiss him again. All the while, my right hand taps the camera icon a few more times, then I drop the phone onto the mattress and focus my attention fully on him again.

"I hope it didn't disappoint," I mumble. "I wanted things to be special. For both of us."

He smiles against my lips. "You're a miracle. I don't want tonight to ever end."

Now I'm smiling as well. It seems we've moved beyond the one night stand stage already. Maybe. Hopefully. I'm hopelessly invested in him, it's why I made possibly every single mistake there is to make when it comes to dating.

"So don't let it," I say.

He rolls onto his back, taking me along with him until I'm propped up, with both arms resting on his chest. Looking down into his eyes, I know that I'm exactly where I'm meant to be. If given half a chance, he'd easily be comfortable enough to sleep on. Whereas the protruding bones in my hips would graze a skinnier lover, his body cushions me; moulding against me so we fit together perfectly.

"You won't tire of me?" he asks, while brushing a lock of damp hair out of my face.

It would be easy to tease him; or to dance around the real issues in this conversation, but I won't. Too much is riding on it for me already.

"That depends," I say. "Will you take me for granted?"

"Never." The look in his eyes disarms me and makes me weak. The skepticism he showed earlier in the evening has faded completely.

"I have something to confess," I say.

His expression turns even more serious. "Yes?"

"I don't generally do this. I mean, things have happened pretty quickly, but I'm not normally this easy."

"I wasn't judging you, if that's what you think."

Although it's the reaction I was hoping for, his words still surprise me. I would have judged me, probably.

"Lust brought us together tonight; that much is undeniable. I already told you that, anyway." I take a deep breath.

He frowns. "But?"

"Shit, don't look so scared! I'm nervous enough as it is." I let out an awkward chuckle.

"Just tell me, then."

"Right. So, yeah, lust. But when you said just now that you didn't want tonight to end, it made me think. I don't want it to end either. Maybe it's not all lust, really."

"Jesus." He exhales deeply and tightens his grip around my lower back. "For a second there I thought you'd changed your mind about all this."

"What? No way!" I rest my head on his chest and readjust my hips, until one leg slips down in between his thighs. It occurs to me that I could get myself off just with one of his thighs if I wanted to.

He's gorgeously soft and squishy all over. I really could get used to this. I so want to.

"You're going to have to be patient with me. I'm clueless when it comes to relationships," he says.

"I haven't been overly successful myself so far either." I run my fingertip up and down across his chest, brushing his hair back and forth in whichever direction I go. "God, I love how furry you are. It's so sexy."

"What were you saying about lust, again?" he teases.

I love how he makes me laugh.

"We talked a lot over dinner. Fine, it was with an audience, but the longer I kept looking at you, the easier it became to forget about the cameras."

"Same here," he says.

"But if there's something you want to know without anyone else watching, please just ask, okay?"

"Okay…"

"Like… I want to know. Have you not had any relationships at all?"

"Not really. Not like this."

To hear him refer to our one very unconventional date as a relationship makes me feel warm and fuzzy inside. I smile and close my eyes, while listening out for his heartbeat.

"Never been in love?" I ask.

"There have been girls I liked. But they were always out of reach. I was always just the friend. A shoulder to cry on; a patient ear."

"Ouch."

He's silent for a while. I wonder what he's thinking about. Finally, his hand travels up my back and neck and starts stroking my hair. It tickles slightly, but in a good way.

"I know I'm not supposed to ask," he starts.

"Ask me anything."

"How many men have you been with? Again, I'm not judging you; I'd *never* judge you. I just…"

"You just want to know," I say.

"It's okay if you don't want to say."

It's not an easy question to ask, or answer. But I promised myself I'd be honest. And he deserves to know what he's getting himself into.

"Promise you won't be jealous?" I ask.

He laughs awkwardly. "Just as long as there's no one

after me, I'll try not to be jealous."

"That's fair. Okay. There have been four before you."

He sighs deeply. "Wow, that's not what I was expecting."

"What did you want to hear?" I counter, while leaning up again and studying his face.

"I don't know, honestly."

"I mean, you weren't expecting to be my first," I say.

"Of course not." He looks away, making it harder for me to get a read on him. "I was kind of expecting more?"

"Because I'm easy?" I pry.

"No, because you're confident. Because you're beautiful and desirable. And that's how the world works. Because I want to imagine you as the sort of person who goes after what they want in life. And actually get it."

"If I'd said two, including you…" I wonder aloud.

"That would have been worse, actually."

My turn to frown. "How so?"

"Because I wouldn't want to hold you back from experiencing things, I guess? I'd think you're settling."

His reactions continue to puzzle me. "Wait, so you're disappointed on my behalf that I didn't sleep around more?"

"Kind of? This doesn't make any sense, does it?"

"Not a lot, no. Your head is a confounding place to be."

"I shouldn't have asked. I'm sorry," he says.

"This conversation does provide much needed context for what I'm about to say, though."

"Which is?" he asks.

"You're the best one out of five by a long stretch. Noone else ever made me feel like this before."

As soon as I've said that, his eyes seek mine out again, and his body seems to tense up underneath me. I feel it in his quickened breaths; in the slightly tighter grip on my back. I see it in the slight parting of his full lips, and the renewed want in his eyes.

"You like the idea of that, don't you?" I whisper.

He doesn't answer, he just continues to stare at me as his hand travels down the small of my back and onto my ass. His fingers dig in, and I grind my crotch against the soft flesh of his upper thigh.

Just like that, I want him again. He runs his fingers up and down the full curve of my ass cheek, and my heart starts racing like crazy.

I can see a pattern developing. Just before our first kiss in the bathroom, we faced some friction, but then we came together spectacularly. His questions about my sex life threatened to annoy me just now; they put me on the spot. But actually, they uncovered a vulnerability; a worry of his, which I'm keen to exploit for our mutual pleasure now.

"I told you to show me what I've been missing all my life earlier. You did just that."

"No." He shakes his head.

I reach down and cup my hand over his balls, squeezing them a couple of times. *Are you ready for round three?*

"You fucked my brains out, Liam."

"I didn't!" He might deny it, but it's the truth.

"You filled me up with that beautiful big cock of yours, and marked me with your jizz. I never let anyone else do that to me. No one else has been inside of me without a condom before."

He groans when I wrap my fingers tightly around his cock. "Oh God."

"Your body gives me more pleasure than anyone else ever has. From the moment I first saw you, I knew I wanted everything you have to give. It's the only way I'll ever be satisfied."

"Shit. Alison," he groans.

"But by your logic, maybe I can't be sure if you want me back, or if you're just settling for me because I happen to be here? How would you know, if you haven't sampled what else is out there?" I ask, while letting go of his cock again, letting it flop down against the bare skin of his fat thighs. *God, I want to ride that fat dick of his.*

He closes his eyes just for a moment, but then opens them again and wraps his hand tightly around the back of my neck.

"I want you, Alison. Don't torture me."

"Torture you? I'm giving myself to you. Look at what you do to me."

I dip down and press my lips against his, while grinding my wet cunt into him. He doesn't say a word, but his eyes speak volumes. His lips devour me; he pulls me against him tightly with feverish need.

"Think I've ever been this wet for another guy? I haven't. I'm not settling," I whisper against his lips.

He grabs my ass again, and shoves me onto his crotch.

For a moment, I was in charge. I was telling him what's what. But although he's on his back, and I'm sitting upright on top of him, he's ready to take over.

"Ride me," he demands.

I smile down at him. "But if you still think I'm only settling, perhaps I should just stop, right?"

"Oh, hell no! This is happening right now," he says.

Just like during our first kiss at the restaurant, he lifts me up with both hands on my hips, only to put me back down on top of his cock. It doesn't quite go in, but the pressure it puts against my clit is enough to make me moan.

So good. So close already.

I lean with one hand against the roundest part of his belly and lift my hips, while redirecting the tip of his dick right where it needs to be.

Love drunk eyes look up at me. This entire scene is plucked straight out of a filthy dream. I intend to relive it again and again with him.

"Look at you. You're so sexy," I whisper. "You're so mine."

I lower myself and close my eyes when his cock stretches me out again. We'll be so sore in the morning for sure. But right now, I'm not going to worry about it, I'm just going to enjoy this.

I start to move, slowly and deliberately. My cunt reacts instantly; tingling and burning with the promise of the pleasure that's to come. His hands still rest on my hips, though his eyes are drawn elsewhere now.

With every move of mine, my boobs swing and jiggle. He can't look away; neither do I want him to. I'm similarly mesmerised by the way his body moves underneath me. The ripples that travel across his large belly when I bring myself down hard onto him. The sway of his big moobs with every stroke.

He reaches for my arm and pulls me down against him. The feeling of his full body ebbing and flowing against my much smaller frame encourages me to get rougher with him. To use him exactly as I see fit.

I take his nipple into my mouth and suck, hard.

His grip on me tightens and he starts to grind his hips upwards into me.

Getting fucked has its own benefits, but right now, with me on top, I get to feel more of his impressive length. Every time I bear down on him, his beautiful cock fills me completely, and still I get to touch, fondle, squeeze and bite as much of his fat torso as I like. I want to bury my face in his chest hair. Run my fingernails across the stretchmarks on his side. Take a bite out of his tit, and suck on the silky soft, hairless skin on the side of his neck until it turns purple and blue. And I do. All of the above.

Meanwhile, he isn't passive about it at all. His hands touch me confidently, like he owns me. Once or twice, he brings his palm down on my ass hard enough to make it sting. His hips buck up into me, pushing for a more feverish pace. His lips try to seek me out, but I'm too short for him to reach, so he just groans and pants into my hair.

We're not making love tonight; we're fucking like animals. But all of it feels so right. So justified. Because I'm his, and he's mine. And after confessing some of the things that probably should have remained secrets, neither of us seems worried about being judged anymore.

"I'm getting close," I stammer through urgent breaths.

"Baby, do it for me," he demands. "I want to see your face this time."

I plant both hands on his chest and raise myself up, all the while bearing down on his hard cock with renewed energy.

My lower abdomen starts to tighten. My mind goes blank and I forget to breathe. I keep slamming down into him. Harder, faster. I reach a new level of high; my body feels light and purposeful all at once. I exist for him. To cum for him.

And he's here for me.

The look in his eyes, a mix of need and admiration, it's enough to start the chain reaction that is my latest and greatest orgasm.

"Oh, fuck yes!" I call out.

Our bodies are slick, both inside and out. This time it's my turn to drip sweat on him.

He manipulates me seemingly without effort; his

strong hands continue to spur me on to go faster. Just like that, I'm done for. I'm conquered.

"Liam, don't stop!" I scream.

He doesn't. While my insides shudder and twist; pleasure washes over me with such force it brings tears to my eyes. I'm lost for words, all I can do is moan while he continues using my tired body; moving me up and down his cock like a sex doll until suddenly - without warning - he erupts too.

"Shit, Alison!" he growls.

I open my eyes again to enjoy his orgasm face. That deep crease between his eyebrows which I'm going to forever associate with pleasure. Those full lips which I know to taste so good. Eyes, mostly shut because he's completely overwhelmed by the moment.

Although I'm utterly destroyed, I still grind down into his crotch as firmly as I can. I want all the cum he has to give; every last drop. I want him to feel better than he ever has before. It's only fair, because that's what he's done for me already. Twice.

He shudders and whimpers underneath me and finally, I too allow myself to collapse onto him. There we remain, silent but for our desperate gasps for air. Two individuals joined as one. Bodies as well as fluids, inseparable and indistinguishable from one another.

Minutes pass, and I finally try to move just a little. To straighten the cramp in my hip, and give him space to recover as well, but he won't have it.

"Stay," he whispers.

"Okay." I snuggle my head against his chest again.

His heart is still racing; we've both gotten a proper workout tonight.

"Alison," he says a little louder this time.

"Yes?"

"I mean it. Don't leave."

Instinctively I know he isn't just talking about right now or even tonight. Once we got that early friction between us sorted out, we ended up on the same page fairly quickly.

"I won't." There's a lot I want to tell him, but I keep it simple and concise for now.

He sighs and loosens his grip on my back, allowing me to slide off him partially and stretch my legs.

"We're going to hurt tomorrow," I remark. In fact, I'm already sore right now.

I glance across the beautifully decorated hotel room at the thing that attracted me to it in the first place. The jacuzzi still remains unused, though I'd filled it up the moment we got here.

We might not have sex in it like I'd envisioned; not this soon, but that doesn't mean we can't enjoy it still.

I lean up onto one elbow and glance down at Liam's face. "What do you say we have a dip?"

He smiles lazily. "You haven't forgotten, huh?"

"Never."

He gestures down at himself. "Do you know how long it takes to dry all this off?"

"You're making it sound like that's a bad thing. I'm up for the challenge."

"It involves getting up, though."

Before even considering if it'll make him uncomfortable, I pat him on his belly. "Come on, get up. It'll soothe our achy muscles."

He tries to reach for me, to pull me back down. "Just a little while longer. I haven't had this much exercise in like, forever."

I escape his grasp fairly easily and slip off the bed.

While looking back, I wink at him. "A lot of fun can be had in water."

Then, I turn my attention to the tub again. Swirls of steam rise from the surface of the water. It's the perfect temperature and looks bloody inviting.

But first… I grab what remains of the bottle of bubbly from the champagne cooler and empty it into the two glasses. I don't care if it's flat by now. After carefully placing them both on the edge, I dip my toe into the water for the first time.

Heaven.

I turn around again. Liam has shifted onto his side and is staring at me from the bed. Enjoying the view of my naked ass, no doubt.

I beckon him over. "You won't want to miss out on this, trust me!"

He smiles and shakes his head, but then he does finally swing his legs over the edge of the bed. I waste no time getting into the tub. The warm water envelops me like a comforting embrace. Not quite as satisfying as Liam's arms have been, but I'm sure I'm eager to add those to the mix shortly as well.

I sink in, allowing the water to creep up to my throat

and close my eyes. It's as good as I had hoped.

The currents are stirred by another presence. I turn around again just as Liam steps in, displacing quite a bit of water.

"It's not going to overflow, is it?" he asks, with a sheepish grin on his face.

I shake my head. "I'm sure there's a drain or something to make sure."

He carefully lowers himself onto the ledge beside me and I can't resist putting my arms around him and floating into his lap.

My lips burn when they brush past his beard to reach his lips. I barely even care. No pain, no gain. His hands draw me in, massaging my tired back and shoulders. He knows just what I need most.

"I'm so glad I came out tonight," I whisper.

"Me too."

I lean back and admire his handsome face. Especially those lips I can't seem to get enough of, no matter how sore I am. And those eyes which appear to mirror my every desire.

Then, I lean across and pick up the glasses of champagne, handing him one.

"Cheers," he says with a smile.

"To us. Because tonight is just the beginning."

"I think I love you," he whispers. "Shit, is that too soon?"

I grin and shake my head. "I was thinking the same thing. I think I love you too."

Just like that, the champagne is forgotten. I hurriedly

put the glass down before being drawn into his arms again. This is where I want to stay. With this beautiful man.

No matter where we are; in his embrace, I am at home.

ABOUT THE AUTHOR

Dear Reader,

If you came across me in real life, you'd never guess the kind of filth I like to read and write. Cleverly disguised as a boring office worker, the drudgery of my 9-to-5 only becomes bearable because of my vivid and explicit imagination. I like fat guys and I cannot lie. In my world, bigger (fatter) is always better. It's been that way for as long as I can remember.

Thanks for reading this story, one of hopefully many of my published sexual fantasies. My stories revolve around one common theme: really big men and the women who can't help but lust for them.

Although I like porn just fine, it's nearly impossible to find it in the flavour that I desire. The written word allows me to explore a world of lush excess that mainstream adult entertainment just cannot provide. When I started writing, I soon discovered the beauty of having a catalog of erotica out there to satisfy my own lustful needs. This is a passion project more than a money-grab.

So, first and foremost, my writing is for me. But perhaps there are other women (or even men) out there who share my tastes; my fetishes and fantasies? My fascination with the larger male form, and sexualisation of food (especially overeating). If that sounds like something you'll wank off to, you've come to the right place.

xxx Hedonist

To find out more, check:

❖ eXplicitTales.com